ALFIE THE WORKER ANT

by Majo

Illustrated by Adrienne Brown

"My name is Alfie and I am a worker ant. I don't have time for fun and games. Life is too serious. I have to be here on the job every day, work hard, and make sure the other ants don't goof off."

One day, while lugging some fruit and not looking where he was going, Alfie bumped into a sweet little ant who was pushing a sugar cube. She had a cute ribbon in her hair with a skirt to match. His heart skipped a beat. Her name was Lily. "Oh! What a beautiful name," he thought.

As you may have guessed, it was love at first sight.

Lily is Alfie's partner now. She loves spending time with him, to sit and do nothing but snuggle and talk about their wonderful future.

"I am a worker ant" said Alfie. " Now that we are starting a family I must work even harder and longer. I don't have time for fun and games. Life is too serious, Lily! But remember, you won't have to worry about anything. I will always take care of you."

Time passed quickly. Soon their little colony grew.

At home, in spite of her busy schedule taking care of their nest, Lily is lonely. She barely ever spends time with Alfie. He would remind her, saying, "I am a worker ant. I don't have time for fun and games. Life is too serious. You wouldn't want me to lose my job, would you? Then what would we do?"

Lily was torn. She didn't want Alfie to lose his job, but perhaps he could find more time to spend with his brood. After all, they were growing rapidly and they hardly even knew him, except for a quick goodbye in the morning and a sleepy goodnight kiss while they were half asleep.

Alfie was always working.

"Good job Alfie!!! You are my best worker. For your wonderful dedication I am going to give you a raise. Look at all the tunnels you have excavated. I know I can always depend on you. You never take time for fun and games. You are a worker ant and you always get the job done right."

Alfie couldn't wait to share this exciting news with Lily.

"Lily, Lily, guess what!!! I got a raise. The boss said I was very dependable. Isn't that wonderful!"

"Yes Alfie, that is good news. By the way, don't forget we're going to the Ant Hill Colony State Fair this weekend."

"Oh Gee. I don't think I can go. I am a worker ant. I don't have time for fun and games. Life is serious. I am needed at the excavation site."

"Yes, Alfie, I understand... but, we need you here."

"Oh, you'll do fine without me."

"But we will miss you", sighed Lily.

"I'll miss you too, but my work must come first. Besides, how could we afford to go to the fair if I didn't have my job?" Alfie replied.

"Alfie, you have been our best employee. You have built our little ant hill into the biggest community in the area. What will we ever do without you? Now, to show our appreciation, please accept this magnificent gold watch in recognition of your long and hard work at the Ant Hill Excavating Company. Also, this plaque is a reminder of all your many accomplishments."

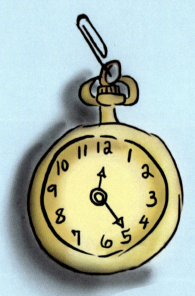

"HELLO!!! Is anybody here? Where is everyone?", called Alfie.

He looked all around.
He checked each room. EMPTY.

Alfie shrugged his shoulders. His excitement turned to sadness. He hung his plaque beside the many pictures of his family. They were all grown up now. Some even had colonies of their own. Alfie looked down at his shiny new gold watch.

"Where did the time go?", he wondered.

He noticed a letter on the kitchen table...

It read: "Alfie, I've gone to visit our relatives. I tried to tell you but you didn't listen. I'll be home tomorrow. I left some food for you... Lily."

Alfie stared at the note for a long, long, time. "She didn't even sign it *LOVE, LILY*... just Lily."

He got up and began to look at the photos on the wall. His plaque looked out of place.

"I did it for them", he said sadly. "I gave them everything they ever wanted. I was a good provider. Lily never had to worry. I was a worker ant. I never had time for fun and games. Life was too serious. I made sure we always had more than enough. I wasn't here very much... but my job gave us security."

"ISN'T THAT WHAT I WAS SUPPOSED TO DO?"

23

"I'll just sit here and wait." he thought.

Alfie looked at his bright, new, gold watch and sighed... "I've got all the time in the world now."

"I wish I had…

    If only I could…

        Is there still a chance?"

"HELLO ALFIE, I'M HOME!!!"

Illustrator

Adrienne Brown was born and raised in Kansas. "So early on in my childhood I was amazed by sketching and doodling". I absolutely loved picture books. As I grew up I collected all I could. I longed to be a children's book illustrator." Most of her career was in graphic design and illustration. "You name it, I have probably drawn it."

She now resides in the Mountains of Idaho with her husband and daughter. Snuggled in the mountains and illustrating as much as possible. "I love the personal collaboration with Majo and creating her characters. Helping her wonderful stories come to life is an incredible feeling. I am truly blessed to be a part of it all."

Contact Adrienne at adbrown14@gmail.com or papermoonco.com

Author Biography

Majo is a wife, mother, grandmother, writer and entrepreneur who promotes positive thinking, and achieving a high quality of life. While raising her family, she began her career as a corporate consultant, training employees in team building, sales and diversity. She also earned a real estate license, wrote a column called "The Family Hour" for a Philadelphia area newspaper and modeled in print and television. She founded three businesses to foster personal accountability, successful parenting and improving the prevalent cultural mindset regarding women in advertising.

Of all her many accomplishments, Majo is most proud of being the Mother of her eight children and grandmother of many. Majo is a beautiful, energetic and determined entrepreneur. She has written seven books for children as well as adults, HUMBLE PIE, THE COOL CHAMELEON, CLEO THE COLD FISH, LESSONS ON FLYING, A DOG AND CAT RELATIONSHIP, THE DRAB CATTERPILLAR, and ALFIE THE WORKER ANT. It has taken her 30 years and many, many rejection letters to achieve this goal. The saying "It's never too late" and Bob Dylan's quote "He who is not busy being born, is busy dying" motivate Majo to keep growing.

Majo is married and lives in Doylestown, PA.

Contact Majo at her website:
MajoTheAuthor.com or email: majo44@aol.com

NOTES